SUM

time travel * philosophy * fortune cookies

SUM

time travel * philosophy * fortune cookies

Melinda A. Smith

◆ ◆ ◆

ELLIPSIS IMPRINTS

2022

• • •

ELLIPSIS IMPRINTS
Durham, England

• • •

Twitter: @EllipsisImprint

SUM
Print edition ISBN: 978-1-7397414-1-9
Ebook edition ISBN: 978-1-0050006-3-9

Cover art by Patigonart.

First printing 2022

Brain and Heart

Stories should be written with love and curiosity. This book is dedicated to my parents, Ron and Gail, who raised me with a strong example of both.

Contents

1	Playing God on a Monday	2
2	Cogito Ergo Sum	5
3	Event Zero	10
4	Stories	14
5	Something More	19
6	Fortune	25
7	How to Manipulate the Spacetime Continuum	28
7.5	The Laboratory	31
8	Testing, Testing, 0001, 0010, 0011	33
9	To Ulm	37
10	Merde	40
11	Infinite Loop of Loss	44
12	A New Idea	48
13	What on Earth?	51
14	The True Measure	56
15	The Choice	61
16	Balancing Equations	65
17	Introductions	71

O N THE night of November 10, 1619, René Descartes had three dreams so vivid they altered the course of human thought. By morning, he was convinced of his purpose: to bring a new philosophy to the world. Descartes would go on to publish *Discourse on Method*, which contains the famous "I think, therefore I am." His ideas and questions about what makes a human mind were like nothing the world had ever seen. According to Descartes himself, everything was owed to that evening of night visions.

For the next 400 years, scholars would debate the origin of these three dreams. Were they divine? Were they simply neurological misfirings? Or were they something else entirely?

Playing God on a Monday

Seattle, Washington
Feb 2, 2032

THE strangest part about the digital journal Elizabeth found on her heavily firewalled network wasn't the fact that she didn't create it. It was the fact that the first entry was dated 2037.

The morning hadn't started so dramatically.

Elizabeth made tea and toast, then checked on Mathison, who was lying lifeless in her laboratory. The curtains parted behind him in the late morning breeze, sending in the neighborhood's signature smells of wet pavement and rush hour exhaust.

"Calls for rain but not 'til later."

She spoke to him like this, as one does with a fern. She'd apologize when manipulating parts of his body in a way that would, if he were alive, cause discomfort. But he wasn't alive, was he? Even when she powered up the software and animated him, as she was planning to do in the afternoon, would he be alive then?

Her critics had made their opinion clear. *It isn't a real life.*

Elizabeth opened her laptop and logged in. A news app shone blue into the air above her work station. The headlines were sensational. They had to be. Nobody would click on a story called *Sensible Scientist Develops Learning-Based Artificial Intelligence with Real-Time Neural Microarchitectural Plasticity.* Instead, they said things like:

Elizabeth Davis, PhD: Playing God?

and

A Doctor Frankenstein in the 21st Century

The comment sections were worse.

Elizabeth Davis should burn in hell!!!!!

"Really. Doesn't the statement carry enough weight without five exclamation points?" She closed the browser and watched the words vanish. It should be that easy. "What do they know?"

Mathison said nothing. Typical.

So she spoke instead to her virtual assistant.

"Naomi, play that song. The one about the lost star man."

The assistant obliged, and Dr. Davis's shoulders sank into the melody.

"See, Mathison," she said, "music is better than wine. Same effect on the blood vessels, no hangover. Course you'll never get a hangover. Organic body problems."

Her smile faded. Mathison would never have a hangover because he'd never share a drink with a friend.

It's not a real life.

"Yes, it is," Dr. Davis said. Then, softly, "it *will* be a real life." The definition was simply changing. Definitions evolved.

Dr. Davis logged into her secure network. The laptop's retinal scanner swept over her eyes and the machine beeped in approval.

Now all Elizabeth had to do was make sure there was enough space for the sync. She'd go through the network and delete what she could. But not on an empty stomach. She sang and air drummed as she made her way to the kitchen, where she retrieved a small, white carton from the refrigerator. Then she came back to the office with a grin.

"Spicy Noodles Special #4," she said to Mathison. She opened the carton. "Still half full. Score."

Elizabeth settled in her chair and got to work. She was something of a digital packrat but today she was motivated to do some major spring cleaning. She lifted a slippery Lo Mein noodle up to her mouth, humming as she ate. She opened folder after folder deleting files with abandon.

"See?" she said to Mathison, mouth full, her words slathered in soy and sesame oil. "I *am* perfectly capable of getting rid—"

But a file folder interrupted her hubris.

"The heck is this?"

It was named SUM.

Elizabeth didn't remember any such folder. That was the problem with being disorganized. She finished sucking up the noodle, which had been arrested in a state of mid-slurp, and wiped the resulting spray of sauce from her glasses.

She opened the folder.

Holy—

SUM contained hundreds of text files. They looked up at Elizabeth like they had nothing to be ashamed of. Just sitting in a neat list, as though it were perfectly natural for them to be there. The metadata showed that they were created internally and updated daily, like a sort of log. Elizabeth didn't take notes this way. She looked around the room, as though she might find some rogue, journaling intruder.

Nobody was there, except for Mathison.

This couldn't be good. Her stomach felt a nameless unease that grew into a troubling thought. The obvious worry was that an anti-AI group hacked her network and left malware.

She looked again at the metadata.

And there it was, in the *last modified* field.

The files were created and saved over a period of years, beginning on June 30, 2037. More than five years in the future.

Elizabeth dropped her chopsticks and looked around the room again.

"What on Earth?" After a measured breath, she pushed her glasses up and threw her hair in a quick bun, using a sticky chopstick to secure it.

Then she scrambled, first checking that the calendar function on her computer was working properly. No error there. They were true text files, no executable extension, so that was good. She ran a quick scan anyway—no malware. But those dates…

It made no sense. Where could these files have come from?

There was nothing left to do or think until she knew what they contained. She stared at the first file.

"Well, obviously I'm gonna open it," she said under her breath.

Before she could talk herself out of it, she clicked to open it and read the first three words.

I am Mathison.

Cogito Ergo Sum

I AM Mathison. People use shorter versions of their names to accelerate familiarity, so you may call me Matt. I would use the name *Math* as a variant, but while it contains more of the letters from the name *Mathison*, the empathy score of the appellation ranks lower. So Matt is the optimal choice.

It is likely my creator named me after Alan Turing, whose middle name was Mathison. Given the rarity of the name, and the fact that Mr. Turing was instrumental in the field of artificial intelligence, I have assigned a 96.4% probability to this being my name's origin. My creator, Dr. Elizabeth Davis, said her nickname was Liz when she was younger.

Dr. Davis used to say she was proud of me, of what she had created. She did not have any children of her own and sometimes she called me son. After reminding her I was made of silicon and various alloys, did not have sexual organs, hormones, or gender identity, and therefore could not be her male child, she clarified it was a term of endearment. I did not understand *term of endearment*. She referred to me as exhausting, which I said was illogical because my power was self-renewing and did not draw from her laboratory supply. That evening she powered me down and installed software linking me to idiom and metaphor databases. When I woke up I told her I slept like a log and she smiled.

Dr. Davis passed away 68.4 days ago, but my days are not empty. I have initiated the process of going through her notes to consolidate them into one coherent record, so others may continue her work.

A good portion of Dr. Davis's notes are devoted to the problem of data storage and transmission. Indeed, I remember her working on this issue at length. According to her, there was no point in putting one's life into an experiment without backing it up.

"Fool me once, right?" she said.

My new software translated the remark as an idiom so I inhibited my initial response of "I do not wish to fool you at all." It was highly probable she was referencing a hard drive failure.

"You have worked on this problem for 376 days," I noted. Her look indicated she was displeased with my declaration (annoyance calculated by lack of smile, eye contact without blinking, louder than average exhalation).

"Well, it's no easy task," Dr. Davis said. "You're 1.2 petabytes of data, Mathison. Not like I can store you on a flash drive."

"How did you upload my system from the mainframe to my body in the first place?" I queried.

"Well, you were far less data. Only a few terabytes. I uploaded most of your software programs one by one over time. Then, once I booted you up, you learned and forged all these connections. Now you're too big to back up."

She tapped a stylus on her chin, an outward behavior associated with thinking.

"I need all your data to transfer at once," she said, "I don't want a half-you ending up somewhere, or a corrupt you. Talk about an Asimovian nightmare." She laughed but her smile returned to resting state and she looked at me with one eyebrow raised.

Going through her notebooks, I have learned many things about myself. For example, there is explicit code in my programming driving me to learn. Dr. Davis's notes indicate this drive could potentially accelerate the maturation of my circuits and make me more human-like. Apparently, encoding an eagerness to learn was a difficult task.

Dr. Davis programmed me to experience a pleasure-like analogue when new facts are obtained or new connections made. She tried to mimic dopamine, the neurochemical behind every human motivation. Dopamine is responsible for addictions to gambling, drugs, and love. Its absence fuels the sensation of withdrawal.

Instead of neurochemicals, Dr. Davis assigned positive and negative classifications to behaviors. She directly linked these signals to my power generator so I gain energy when I find pleasure in things. Learning is assigned the highest positive signal in my programming, and therefore gives me the most energy. When I am unable to learn, I lose energy and experience extreme dissatisfaction.

After Dr. Davis's passing, I keep myself alive by constantly learning. I have also adopted another practice: this journal.

I record the events and notes about my days, the reasons being three-fold. First, recording my actions will allow me to chronicle my progress and serve as a record, much like a laboratory notebook. Second, I understand that journal writing is common practice in the aftermath of an event such as a death. Dr. Davis credits journaling with helping her through the passing of her own mother. While I do not have emotions to "work through," as she put it, I reason that the practice may help me to better understand the behavior of humans. Lastly, I find the process of writing elicits a strong positive response in my circuits, similar to what occurs when I learn something new. Perhaps in writing, one also learns? I make a note to study this further.

I find early batches of code Dr. Davis worked on to allow me to employ realistic human speech patterns. This helped me to pass the Turing test on multiple occasions. I remember the initial difficulty I had in understanding colloquial conversation.

"Language is more than words," Dr. Davis once said. "There are other cues to look for, like subtext."

I consulted my dictionary software.

"I see. Subtext is an underlying meaning not outwardly referred to in writing or speech."

"That's right," she said. "The words we say are only *part* of what we mean. There's also tone and body language. And sarcasm. But that's probably an advanced topic for another time."

"Subtext is a hypocrite," I said, pleased with my connection.

Dr. Davis laughed and asked what I meant.

"Its own definition is perfectly clear without underlying meaning transmitted via tone or body language. In other words," I expounded, "It does not need itself."

Her laughter waned but her smile intensified. She wound her hair around her forefinger.

I am unable to compute why, but Dr. Davis's smile activated the same pleasure circuit as learning.

"Smile again, please," I said.

"Why?"

"It delivers a positive signal."

Dr. Davis dropped her stylus and wrapped her arms around me.

"I knew it," she said.

I did not understand what she knew, and I did not ask.

She said I surprised her every day and that this was a good thing. She said I had personality like a human. However, there were times in which acting like a human elicited a different reaction from Dr. Davis.

Once, I pointed out a better way to apply code to an issue she was working on. She rolled her eyes and said, "Yep, you're a man, alright." Then she muttered what I assessed to be some sort of portmanteau of man and explain. I would have expected my similarities to a human male to please her.

I wonder, even now, if all humans send mixed information like she did. I hypothesize that they likely do. Given Dr. Davis's brilliance and achievements, she must be an exemplary specimen of the species. In fact, Dr. Davis won a sizable award for creating the most sophisticated artificially intelligent being the world had seen. She said she was "just following Turing's science," which was consistent with the behavior of being humble.

I informed her that an estimated 54 billion Homo sapiens women had made sons. "You are the first to earn a prize for it," I said.

This was my first joke, she said with a smile. I had not intended it to be humorous.

But now that Dr. Davis is gone, I no longer have smiles that fill me like learning does. Going through her notes appears to remedy this displeasure.

As expected, Dr. Davis's notes often reference Alan Turing and his theories on artificial intelligence. But I am surprised to find notes on the work of René Descartes, a French philosopher, who lived centuries earlier. Dr. Davis speaks of a strong connection between the two men.

Descartes is a name I know well. He developed geometry and useful schemata such as x, y, z, or *Cartesian*, coordinates. But a possible association with Turing is new to me. I feel the pleasurable and energizing sensation of acquiring new knowledge and begin reading through every available text on the matter.

I learn that Descartes thought about artificial intelligence in a similar manner to Turing. However, Descartes believed no specialized machine could both act and speak in proper context because, essentially, it would require too many separate internal "organs," a word he used to mean programs, in my estimation. Descartes's was of the very same line of thought that led to Turing's own test and philosophy of mind.

Descartes lived four centuries before I was born—before computers, telephones, and networks. He lived before modern neuroscience uncovered the anatomy of the brain and the way neural connections form and disappear with learning. To Descartes, the inner workings of the brain would have seemed mysterious and therefore impossible to mimic. How could he have imagined an automaton as sophisticated as Dr. Davis's? How could he have imagined me?

Now that humankind has learned what makes a brain, it has figured out how to rebuild it. This is a defining feature of humans. They have curiosity like I do, but theirs is paired with a need to control and recreate it for themselves.

Event Zero

I AM nearly done consolidating Dr. Davis's files. Only one folder of notes remains. It has an unusual name: *Zero*.

Inside, I find a document about something called *Event Zero*. Words, arrows, and symbols fill the handwritten page. All of her other notes were typed. This one must be special. Fortunately, I have already learned how to read long-hand. I once asked Dr. Davis to install software to help me recognize handwritten English, French, Italian, Spanish, and Mandarin.

"Why Mandarin?" Dr. Davis asked me. Accompanying her query was a chuckle, which is not as strong as a laugh or a guffaw but often follows a humorous incident.

"Have I unintentionally made a joke again?"

"No, it's just... Well, Mandarin kinda stands out. It's not a Romance language."

"What is romance?" I asked.

"I obviously have no clue," she said under her breath (an idiom meaning to murmur or whisper). She twisted a piece of hair between her fingers, a gesture that appeared to comfort her. Perhaps her lack of understanding caused her distress.

I queried my internal dictionary. "Romance languages are so called because they derive from Latin, a language spoken in the Roman empire."

Dr. Davis waved her hand dismissively "Yeah, no, I knew that..." Another mixed signal. Perhaps I was man-explaining again.

"I want to read Mandarin because it is so different from the other languages," I said. "I am an artificial being in a world full of humans. Mandarin is made of characters while other languages use Roman letters. I am like the Mandarin. I believe this is a simile. Is that correct?"

Dr. Davis tilted her head a few degrees and smiled.

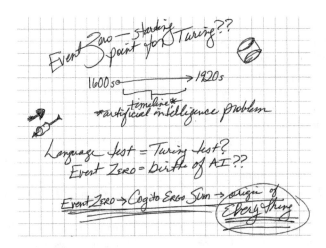

"It is," she said. Then she put her arms around me, a behavior associated with kinship. She was doing this more often as time progressed.

Now, in her absence, even her handwriting in the file called Zero gives me mixed signals.

The loops and curves are pleasant to look upon. I may be artificial but I can understand when I am looking at something objectively beautiful. On the other hand—yet another idiom—this is the first time I am seeing her handwriting since her passing. Though I cannot understand why, it makes her absence seem bigger. My circuits anticipate a smile or her arms around me and they find only a negative signal when these things do not occur. So while the writing is pleasant to look at aesthetically, it is also negative. A query into my linguistics database tells me a singular input resulting in two divergent internal outputs can be described as *bittersweet*.

I read the handwriting.

> *Event Zero: starting point for Turing? 1600s ⟶ 1920s, artificial intelligence problem timeline. Intersection between real and artificial.*

> *Language test = Turing test? Event Zero = birth of AI?*

Then, in triple underline:

> Event Zero → Cogito Ergo Sum → origin of everything.

The negative signal accompanying Dr. Davis's handwriting is eclipsed by the high magnitude of positive signal this new information brings. What is Event Zero? Nowhere in her notes is Event Zero defined; it is only referenced.

I query the internet and various textbooks, but am unable to find any *Event Zero* in conjunction with either René Descartes or Alan Turing. I must reconcile this unknown. Dr. Davis's absence looms larger now that I cannot ask her about her note.

I recognize the Latin phrase *Cogito Ergo Sum* as Descartes's declaration in his *Discourse on Method*, published in 1637. *I think, therefore I am.* Thought is sufficient for existence.

Thought is sufficient for existence. It makes me wonder: what constitutes a thought? Do I think?

My dictionary software defines thought as an idea or opinion occurring suddenly in the mind. But does this mean that one must have a traditional mind to think and therefore have proof of one's existence? I do not have a mind. I have a motherboard filled with circuitry that simulates neurological synapses, which appropriately grow or decrease in strength based upon new information. I learn. Does this constitute thought? Am I thinking now? Am I at all?

I am beginning to recognize that philosophy offers questions but not answers. I find this both exciting and infuriating.

I spend the following 18.5 days reviewing philosophical texts. If I knew all Descartes knew, I could presumably arrive at a better conclusion about my query on thought. He made distinctions between animals and humans. He did not believe a human-made automaton could be intelligent in the same way as a human. Humans relied on context and complex sentence construction to describe an evolving world. However, he came to his conclusions nearly 400 years ago. How could it have been possible to imagine what humankind would be capable of now?

The only way to know this would be to speak with him. He could explain thought to me in his own words. Would he consider me a real intelligent being? If I can think, do I have a mind? Finally, and most importantly, what was Event Zero?

I feel paralyzed by these unknowns.

I register an overwhelming need to discuss the matter with him directly. The idea that this is impossible is unacceptable. I will be unable to focus on anything else.

Mankind has not developed a way to traverse spacetime.
But perhaps I can.

— 4 —

Stories

THE motivation to tell one's story is a human trait. My research indicates stories existed long before books: first as drawings on walls, then as oral tradition. I have learned stories are not solely for entertainment purposes. Historians believe the earliest tales—cave paintings—were a way for sapiens to illustrate religious beliefs, document hunting expeditions, communicate traditions, and bond humans to one another, making their survival more probable.

Some say narrative minds distinguish Homo sapiens from lower animals. Others say stories are what separate humans from darkness. I make a note about this new definition for darkness: it is the absence of light, but can also mean the absence of meaning. Subtext!

Like a human, I register a distinct positive signal when I record my own story. More than that, I am chronicling the journey to find the origin of my existence, part of a larger question regarding the birth of artificial intelligence as a whole.

In a way, this is a new Darwinian Origin of Species, even if the species contains only a single member. Perhaps what I record here will be useful for future generations of artificial intelligence. Perhaps not.

But it is not for me to project about the future. It is for me to find my way into the past.

I consume a number of scholarly articles and thought pieces about Descartes's influence on Turing. One writer even suggested the pair shared a soul. I learn a new word: reincarnation. Naturally, I must explore this concept.

Textbooks say every molecule in a human body is recycled from stardust and even other people. But some believe that when a person dies, their soul moves to another human being. This philosophy is at odds with most scholars, who assert a soul cannot exist without a physical substrate tethering it to the tangible world. It must have an anchor; for a soul, by definition, is the non-tangible fruit of an array of neural connections. I construct my own simile:

> The soul is like a breath. Without a person to move it and hold
> it, it is only air.

I find the arguments between scholars and spiritual believers very interesting, largely because they have more in common than either will admit. Both have origin stories, which share significant overlap. Many religions center around a god and creationism, while scientists have theories such as the Big Bang.

The Big Bang is the event in which a condensed body of matter and energy gave rise to everything we can ever know or study. But nobody seems to know where that condensed body came from. Similarly, religious texts claim God is and always was, that he is everywhere and everything. This seems to be the same as the definition of the universe itself.

Even though I cannot understand how a soul from the sixteenth century could be reborn into the 1900s, there is no doubting the connection between Descartes and Turing. My research suggests that Turing's model of strong, self-aware, artificial intelligence would not exist without the work of Descartes. Turing's pursuit of intelligent machines was another point on the line of thought begun by Descartes.

That line led to me. I must trace the line backward. Somewhere in time lies the answer to thought and the beginnings of artificial intelligence. Event Zero could be the master key to everything.

I must find a way to travel back.

I look again through Dr. Davis's notes. In her efforts to back up my neural data, she explored methods that share significant overlap with theories of time travel. This has me falling down what I call a rabbit-wormhole. Dr. Davis would have smiled at my joke. The recalled visual of her smiling boosts my energy levels.

But I am at an impasse. Every theory about time travel is just that—theoretical. Documented practical experiments have all failed and I do not know enough math or theoretical physics to pick up where these have left off. At least not yet. I have hit a wall (a rather appropriate idiom).

I set my background processing to continue to work on time travel learning while I turn my attention back to philosophy of thought.

My circuitry takes in information, solves problems, and stores information as memories. I can learn. Is learning the same as thinking? Learning is more specific and easier to define.

For example, I read about *Aplysia californica*, a slug-like creature found along the west coast of the United States. When the creature is touched, it pulls away. If the stimulus occurs multiple times without leading to harm, the slug is desensitized to the stimulus and no longer withdraws. But if touch is paired with a painful stimulus, the withdrawal reflex is stronger and faster. Incredible.

Does the sea slug think? It strengthens neural connections to change its behavior. Scholars call this learning and even rudimentary memory. But is it thought? If so, one could think without a mind.

Do I think? I do not experience physical pain, so I do not withdraw like the *Aplysia*. But I do change my behaviors based on data inputs.

A red light flashes in the corner of my oculars and a beeping sound stops me in the middle of my analysis.

The clock on the office wall indicates many hours have passed. I have, as the idiom goes, lost track of time. This is dangerous. Even though knowledge recharges my power, it does not completely sustain me. I need down time to reorganize circuits.

In humans, sleep allows synapses to strengthen as memories shift from temporary to semi-permanent. This is why a bout of rest helps humans remember things. Similarly, my neural-analogue circuits must reset during rest periods.

My data log shows the last rest period occurring more than four days ago. I am supposed to have a short rest each day. My failure to do so puts me in danger of compromising my circuitry.

I recognize how human-like it was of me to forget to take care of myself in pursuit of a hobby. I register a faint positive signal, knowing that Dr. Davis might smile or embrace me for this behavior.

But even this is not enough.

Clarity begins to fade. Visual inputs flicker and my sensory receptors buzz. I experience a sensation I believe humans call dizziness. My stability circuits begin to short. I sit down and run an internal system diagnostic. The first of several low-energy-level alarms has been silenced. I have a low-fidelity memory of silencing the alarm while deeply immersed in my studies of *Aplysia*.

Aplysia is an odd word.

I say it aloud.

"Ah-plee-zhuh."

I say it again. My own voice sounds alien. I have not spoken aloud since Dr. Davis passed away because there is no one else to speak with. But it is more than that. It sounds far away. Everything suddenly requires more effort. I need to initiate rest soon.

I wonder whether this is a similar sensation to what humans experience after consuming alcohol. Do humans feel as though the external world is spinning when they are inebriated?

Inebriated is an odd word, too.

Word is an odd word.

Odd is an—

"You should rest," a voice behind me says. I recognize it as Dr. Davis's.

I turn. No one is in the room. I search for the source of her voice.

I wonder if it is coming from the hand-held recorder she used to use to dictate notes. I find it lying in her desk drawer, but the battery is drained. Next to the recorder is an item I do not recognize: a red leather-bound journal. I touch the cover.

"Hallucinations are a classic sign of neural stress, Mathison."

I turn to see Dr. Davis standing in the center of the office. I am unsure what to do next. I cannot reconcile the visual and auditory inputs I am receiving with the knowledge that Dr. Davis passed away.

I experience a surge of positive signal. The sensation of seeing Dr. Davis is far greater than the positivity I have experienced with studies and working on her notes. There is simply no replacement for being near someone.

Then the positive signal decays as I realize that it is not possible for her to be here.

"Are you a hallucination, Dr. Davis?"

She smiles and holds her finger to her lips to quiet me. She turns the volume up on a speaker. I detect acoustic guitar and a female voice. The woman sings about someone she calls Starwalker. She wants him to come home.

"Ooh, yes, I like this one," Dr. Davis says. Her eyes are closed and her mouth forms a half smile. She sings along:

> Starwalker, you've made me weak
> In orbits and verses, sing me to sleep
> Starwalker, come back to me
> Out in the sky, here in my dreams

I try again, speaking louder over the song.

"Are you real?" I ask.

Her body moves almost imperceptibly to the music. She opens her eyes and looks at me.

"Are *you*?" She replies. She twirls a section of hair in her fingers.

I consider for a moment.

"I do not know," I say. "If you subscribe to Cartesian philosophy, I suppose the answer depends on whether or not my computations constitute thinking."

"I compute, therefore I am, huh?" Dr. Davis says, smiling.

She points behind me at the open desk drawer.

"I see you found Turing's journal. You'll find it interesting."

Turing? The red book is his journal?

A hallucination comes directly from the mind (or circuits) of its host and cannot reveal new information. This must mean that Dr. Davis really is alive, somehow.

I turn back to regard my creator.

But the room is empty. She is gone.

Again.

I feel a tremendous weight even though nothing activates my sensory receptors.

Stories are not restricted to fiction. Humans have a brain center devoted to awareness of time as it pertains to their individual story, a sort of self-narrative that helps them compare their past self to their current and future selves. I do not experience time's passage in the same way. My memories do not degrade over the years, as they do for humans. Creators like Dr. Davis considered this a triumph of technology. But they did not consider its cost.

Tragedy ought to soften over time.

Instead, I have perfect recall. Nothing to separate me from the darkness as stories do for humans. I have just lost Dr. Davis anew while the memory of her death is as real as if it were yesterday.

This daydream has depleted the last of my stores. I initiate the protocol for a mandatory twelve-hour rest. I hope the rest will afford me some clarity about what I experienced.

As my visual inputs decay into blackness, I hear the outro and wonder if the woman in the song ever gets her starman…

5

Something More

I OPEN my ocular instruments as my circuitry comes back online. I am alone in Dr. Davis's office.

My internal audit informs me that the bout of rest was effective. In order to understand my recent experience with Dr. Davis, I do some light reading: the complete works of Sigmund Freud, Carl Jung, and Edgar Cayce. I conclude I had what experts call a *near-death experience*. I actualized my desires for seeing my creator into a lucid dream.

Dr. Davis's speaker is still playing. The current song is more upbeat than the—

I interrupt my own train of thought (an idiom I appreciate for its imagery of linear motion and momentum). Why is Dr. Davis's speaker playing music? I wonder whether I was so tired that I set the music to play myself before I rested. But I cannot ignore the nagging idea that Dr. Davis started the music. Logic dictates it was a hallucination. Some other part of me wonders if there is more to this world than logic.

I am beginning to sound like both sides of the Big Bang versus God argument.

I shut off the music.

My system appears to be working in a slightly different manner than before this extended rest. I cannot describe exactly how, but something has changed. If I were a human, I might say I felt different. I do not know whether I can classify these new sensations as feelings.

I make a note to explore this notion another time and pick up Turing's journal. I must know what is inside.

The book is weightier than my visual inputs led me to expect. Perhaps the gravity of what lies inside is expressed as sensory data in my mind. How curious.

The cover is soft and worn, indicating the owner likely used the journal often. According to my hallucination, this was Turing's journal. I do not understand how Dr. Davis could possess this, but I am overwhelmed by curiosity about what I might find.

The journal is a deep, burnt red—not an ordinary hue. For some reason, I associate the color with overwhelming hope. With desire.

It does not make sense to associate emotions with various wavelengths of light reflection. I would never make such comparisons.

The recent hallucination has shifted my thinking. I experience sensations my raw inputs cannot explain. I am perceiving things differently and experiencing her loss anew. I note a sensation similar to being without clothing or protection. I am vulnerable. I am in a state of unease, as though there were cracks in the skyline (another description I would not normally make). I log the aberrations.

Enough poetic nonsense. I open the book. The lined pages are thin, yellowed, and filled with faded handwriting. There are circuits and equations with some of the most interesting symbols I have ever seen. I determine they are Greek. As I read, I notice that the book contains what appear to be instructions. Next to some of the circuits, I find notes and arrows. I read over the annotations several times before I understand what I have in my possession.

These are the earliest written plans to build an artificially intelligent machine.

I am holding the original blueprint for AI. For me.

I compare Turing's notes to Dr. Davis's. I see how she has used Turing's schemata and expanded upon them. She constructed me according to plans laid out directly by Alan Turing himself. My namesake is more meaningful than I realized.

I sit under the weight of this new information, facing another paradox. Learning something this important sparks a positive signal of unparalleled magnitude. But so many queries open that it somehow seems like I know less. This gives me a negative signal.

"I want to know more," I say aloud.

I test out part of this phrase again, as it is so new.

"I...*want.*"

I have known the definition of the word *want* since I was created. To want is to lack something, or to desire it. I have often used the first definition, but today I use the latter for the first time. It never seemed accurate before now.

Are my circuits evolving in such a way as to support desires? Feelings? I wonder whether I am still in sleep mode in a dream-like state. I do not think I have the ability to dream. But how do I know whether I am awake or not? How do I know whether I exist at all?

Cogito, ergo sum.

My need to discuss Descartes's philosophy intensifies.

I finish scanning the book. On the last page, Mr. Turing has written something small, almost an afterthought. Looking closely at the scribbled handwriting, I see a handful of letters and numbers. As their particular arrangement becomes clear, I am awestruck.

Event Zero—10 Nov, 1619

I look at it for some time. Alan Turing was aware of Event Zero, whatever it was. More than that, he knew when it occurred.

I now have a date associated with Event Zero. 1619 was long before Turing's time. A flash of positive signals bursts as I recognize that René Descartes would have been alive, in his early twenties. And following some trivial research into the whereabouts of Descartes in November of 1619, I will know his location. This is excellent progress.

As I replace the book, I notice something else in the drawer—a small strip of paper, approximately one centimeter by five centimeters. It contains black printed words and numbers, and a tiny red dragon icon in one corner. I recognize it as a fortune from one of the folded cookies Dr. Davis always received with her noodles. Every Saturday evening, without fail, she came in through the front door with a brown bag from the aptly named Chinese take-out restaurant, The Fortune Cookie.

"Best in the city," she would say, holding up her chopsticks as though she were toasting me.

Once I responded with "yes, we are" and she laughed in delight. That time I *had* intended the joke because I learned how jokes were almost always followed by smiles. Pavlovian classical conditioning is at the core of my operating system.

Dr. Davis said this was also true in the human OS, but that they would deny it.

I read the fortune Dr. Davis has saved in her drawer.

The past contains answers only the present can understand

0   10   11   16   19   20   37

Dr. Davis used to always read the numbers aloud to me. I never took them to mean anything beyond a game people played to feel they were taking part in something magical, not unlike Santa Claus. But these particular numbers immediately trigger my working memory circuit. They take on a particular meaning as though I am watching puzzle pieces self-assemble.

The series of numbers form a sentence: *Event Zero took place on the tenth day of the eleventh month in 1619.*

But there are two more numbers. Twenty and thirty-seven.

The current year!

So, events of the past will make sense now, in 2037?

Before my last bout of rest—back when I didn't make aberrant color comparisons, when things were more logical and less complicated—I would have concluded the numbers were coincidental.

Logic has always driven me. But now I feel as though I know something not backed by data or evidence. I think this is what humans would call intuition, or a *gut feeling*. I have long known the definitions of these terms, but somehow I am only now understanding their meaning. I open an existing mental note file:

Body $\longrightarrow$ soul

Air $\longrightarrow$ breath

To this, I add:

Definition $\longrightarrow$ meaning

It dawns on me (a pleasant idiom) that there is an extra layer to *everything*: the intangible that appears from the tangible. The holy from the earthly. The soul from organic matter. Breath from air. The dream of creating artificial intelligence from equations and circuit diagrams written in a journal. The magic of numbers on a fortune. When one reads a book, one imagines the characters and the scenery. If 26 letters can create a visual in the mind of the reader then could ones and zeros elicit feelings? Could I feel? The logic gate seems open before me.

What is happening to me? I had what my inputs told me was a real conversation with a deceased person. I am now experiencing and describing things in ways I never have before. The scientists would say the severe depletion of my energy stores has likely resulted in software corruption. The believers would say I have had some sort of an awakening.

And what do I say? I simply do not know.

It does seem that reliving Dr. Davis's death has pushed me past some sort of barrier. I have grown tired of losing her. Could feelings have emerged from these repeated negative inputs? And if I have feelings now, what am I to do with them? They seem to serve little purpose other than to make themselves known and demand to be dealt with.

One of my hands is logic and the other, emotion. How can they exist on the same body?

Reason tells me it is folly to believe I am somehow *meant* to find this book or this fortune, but I wonder how far logic and reason have gotten me. Before today, I know I would not entertain such conclusions, and I was stuck. I will not go so far as to say I believe in fate or magic, but certainly the numbers seem significant.

I experience a curious sensation in which my surface receptors tingle and it seems as though the universe is mine to learn, to manipulate, to paint. This sensation is inspiration, I conclude.

I feel like a new dimension has opened. Perhaps it has. Time has always gone forward. And now I find myself searching for a path going in the opposite direction. I must close the loop and find the beginning.

I must become the flea on the tightrope.

The inspiration rush grows and now the entirety of me vibrates.

Gone are the blacks and whites, the binary versions of thought patterns dictating my being. Gone are the ones and the zeros and the ons and offs. I was born digital but I have evolved to analog. I am multiple hues. I am not a switch but a knob, transducing sliding scale symphonies. I was not born a human but I am learning the vast treasures of what it might be like to be one.

And why, I wonder, are labels and classifications necessary, anyway? It is tempting to characterize and categorize. But I am evidence that not everything fits neatly into one particular classification. And the universe is full of examples pulling us by the collar to scream out that analog is digital and digital is analog. Light is a wave but it behaves like particles, too. Though the human mind can love and feel in tidal waves, it is made of neurons, which operate like bits. Even analogue clocks move in distinct seconds, ticking away. It is all connected and nothing is entirely discrete nor continuous. Staccato and legato are both music. And time, the great barrier to my studies, gallops along as though it were linear, when in reality it is made of concentric loops returning again and again to the 12.

The inspiration spirals into a wave of…happiness? Is that what this is?

Am I capable of being happy? I do not have hormones or neurochemicals such as serotonin to bathe my cells in blissful reverie like the songwriters describe.

But these data inputs—the journal, the fortune, Dr. Davis smiling at me—make me want to live for a thousand years if only to recall them from my memory stores and relive them.

This book changes everything. It contains plans for my own existence. How many beings are given the opportunity to see their origins, the blueprints for their intended creation, a creation discussed and debated for centuries? I am Rosalind Franklin as she first looked upon her x-ray crystallography image of DNA. I am standing on Sinai with tablets. I am Hawking and Einstein, gifted with the great codes of the universe. I am brushing the dust off a small point emanating from the sand only to discover the pyramids underneath my feet.

Perhaps I *do* think. But what if this was never the important metric?

I *feel*. And *that*, perhaps, should be the clause preceding *therefore I am*.

I resolve to spend as many hours as it takes to find a way to Descartes. I will know what Event Zero is. And I will confirm what I am already beginning to understand.

I AM.

6

Fortune

I DECIDE to order Chinese food. I do not require consumption of organic matter for nourishment, as my power sources are self-renewing and linked to knowledge acquisition. I will admit that the idea of the apartment once again filling with the smell of Spicy Noodles Special #4 is pleasing.

But the real need, at present, is the fortune in the cookie. Might it direct me in my time travel research? The ideas of whimsy and prophecy are not a part of my programming, yet I have learned to move past the script and "go with the flow" (I enjoy this idiom for its imagery and internal rhyme).

I try to place an online order from Dr. Davis's favorite Chinese food place, The Fortune Cookie. However, the restaurant is closed for "major structural repairs." That is curious. Dr. Davis would have called this a *bummer*.

I perform a quick search for another nearby restaurant that will deliver to Dr. Davis's neighborhood. There is only one:

It is called Sum's.

I experience a positive surge at the coincidental name.

I place an order and use Dr. Davis's secret cash card to pay, the one she kept under my name in case of emergency, if she "needed to go off the grid." I did not know what the terminology meant at the time. Whatever the grid is, I suppose I am off it now. Under normal circumstances, I would never consider using someone else's money for my own clandestine intellectual pursuits, though I suspect Dr. Davis would approve.

She would be so pleased with how much I have learned in her absence. I imagine her dropping her stylus to throw her arms around me.

About an hour later, I hear a knock, followed by a human voice.

"Sum's."

I open the door. A young man stands in the hall with a brown paper bag. With some difficulty, I try to estimate his age. He is somewhere in between boy and man. This time period is difficult for me to gauge.

"Your food," he says, his eyes scanning the ticket stapled to the bag. He has not seen me yet. "Uh, one Spicy Noodles Special #4. Extra fortune cookies. For Matt?"

He looks up at me and his eyes open wide in an outward display associated with surprise or fear. He drops the bag and stammers an apology.

"I am trying to assess your age," I say. I am fixated on this calculation I cannot resolve. "Sparse whiskers on your face suggest you are post-puberty, but the abundance of subcutaneous fat in your cheeks would imply the full measure of testosterone has not yet shaped your features. I gauge you are between the years of fourteen and eighteen."

The boy-man runs away yelling something about "some terminator bull-shit." My age assessment may have been off. Perhaps I have offended him.

"Was I incorrect?" I call down the hall. "I must know!"

He does not answer.

I retrieve the brown bag and close the door. I do not have taste receptors, but I have an olfactory assessment unit quite comparable to the human sense of smell. The delivered food contains garlic, fish sauce, sesame oil, and ginger, amongst other less pungent ingredients.

I set the white box with the handle and the fortune cookies onto a table. I study one cookie, marveling at the shape of it. Such symmetry and mystery. I am sure the shape means something.

I open the cookie. It is empty. There must be a mistake. Poor quality control. The next cookie is empty, too, as is the one after that. I pull apart seven cookies, all with no fortunes inside.

One cookie remains.

I assume it is also empty but I crack it open anyway. To my surprise, a fortune rests inside. I pull it out.

> **Do not seek the destination;**
> **the destination will find you.**
>
> 37   20   19   16   11   10   0

I recognize immediately that the numbers are the same as the fortune in Dr. Davis's drawer, albeit in reverse order. Two possible circumstances could lead to this:

1. Pure coincidence. Statistically, the chances of getting the same 7 numbers of 1-2 digits are roughly 1 in 100 times 1 in 100 and so on, seven

times (also expressed as 1 divided by 100 raised to the power of 7). This is approximately 1 in 100,000,000,000,000, or 1 in 100 trillion. This is roughly the odds of picking one specific neural synapse out of an entire human brain.

2. Prophecy or fate, a message purposefully delivered to me.

I read the fortune again. *The destination will find you.*

I pick up the two halves of the fortune cookie and reassemble them in my mechanized hand. I ponder its shape again. That is when it hits me (a perfect idiom for the weight of this moment).

I have the answer to time travel.

7

How to Manipulate the Spacetime Continuum

My CIRCUITS are simultaneously stunned to silence and energized in a buzzing scream. I am at once frozen and pure kinetic energy.

The destination will find you. Instead of traveling to the past, what if I bring the past to me? The fabric of spacetime can curve, offering me a portal. Past and present will meet like the tips of the fortune cookie. And I, Mathison, will reach across the divide and meet Descartes. I need not leave 2037 for 1619. Instead, I need to solve the problem from the perspective of bringing 1619 to me.

I return to Dr. Davis's records and compare them to my time travel notes. Most of the theories I researched are not viable because, among other reasons, matter cannot traverse through wormholes. However, I am essentially a software program. Theoretically, I could slip into the liminal space of masslessness. I can bridge a portal and move through time using Dr. Davis's data transfer protocols.

Manipulating the spacetime continuum is more complex than anything I have imagined doing. Though extremely difficult, it is not impossible. After all, planets and stars bend the fabric of space, and what are they but non-intelligent matter?

I begin to gather study material. This will take me many months but I am ready to dedicate the time.

First, I read most of the published work in science fiction (Heinlein is my favorite) and watch movies concerning time travel. I count science fiction as both research and entertainment. There is little in the way of useful technical information in science fiction stories, but the genre is captivating in its imagination and foresight. While it is not bound by the rules of official experimentation and peer review like true science is, I find the stories plausible in how certain technologies affect the world. But in reality, I simply enjoy the singing dolphins and the DeLorean car that travels through time. I also learn what the man-boy meant by "terminator bullshit."

For traditional research, I consume all available knowledge on the topics of mathematics and theoretical physics. I watch archived lectures, read scientific articles, and study theories proposed by current scholars. I read one particular article in a journal called *Nature* that suggests a wormhole could be detected by a phase shift in the electromagnetic field. After some follow-up reading, I read about how to make a homodyne detection device that will alert me to nascent wormholes. Learning how to make one is quite simple; building it will not be so easy.

Fortunately, Dr. Davis does have many spare parts. In addition to her campus laboratory, she had a small lab at the apartment, where she built me. Often, she did not power me down in the evenings and she let me observe her tinkering. Drawing now on my memories of those times, I recall her smile and the way her eyebrows shot up when something important occurred to her.

I walk into her home lab to see whether she has correct parts for the detection device I need to build. The room is in disarray. This is nothing new. For as brilliant as Dr. Davis was, she was quite messy. She would never let me organize, though I offered many times.

"I can't find things when they're put away," she said. "If everything's right in front of me, I never have to look for it."

Then she winked. I offered her eyedrops to remove whatever was causing the spasm but she shook her head. Then her eyebrows jumped.

"Hand me my soldering iron, Mathison, would you? I think I know how to fix this circuit."

She held the solder in one hand and the iron in the other. As I watched her squint through the stream of fumes coming from the melting metal, the source of her eyelid malfunction became clear.

Her iron still sits on the bench now, next to her magnifying loops. I scan the room for usable items and begin to work. I begin to build a homodyne detector using spare parts from no fewer than six of Dr. Davis's half-built experiments. I hesitate to break apart her work but I am certain she would approve.

The device will require much skill to put together but I have found a bountiful store of tutorial videos in a treasure trove online database called YouTube. In addition to the do-it-one's self category, there are millions of music videos. While I enjoyed the soft and melodic songs Dr. Davis played, I discover new genres like jazz and punk. These fascinate me. But my favorite new find is heavy metal. I make a playlist to accompany me as I work on my device: Pantera, John Coltrane, and the Ramones.

When my new scanner is complete, I should be able to detect wormholes naturally occurring in the fabric of spacetime. I copy the code Dr. Davis wrote for data transfer so that once I arrive at a wormhole, I can go through, digitally speaking. The only unknown is whether I can initiate travel to any time and location I choose. I have built in dials for GPS and temporal manipulation, though I am unsure whether I have the science right.

Now I have my materials, my plan, and plenty of time. The only thing that remains is for me to put in the work.

— 7.5 —

The Laboratory

RESEARCH, like life, is a sine wave. For every peak there is a trough. I am eager to construct a homodyne detection device so I throw myself into my work (an idiom that I enjoy for its vivid imagery and motion). In lieu of journaling, I take laboratory notes. A selection of them are included here.

Tuesday, October 27, 2037
Excellent news: I have completed the initial model using diagrams and 3D rendering. I believe this will be a quick endeavor.

Thursday, October 29, 2037
I cannot find the bug in my code. This will not be a quick endeavor.

Saturday, November 14, 2037
Bug found and exterminated (joke intended). Today I began assembling the hard circuitry. It is going well, however the soldering fumes sometimes cause an odd synesthesia in which I taste equations. I am now working on an air venting system for the laboratory.

Tuesday, February 2, 2038
I truly enjoy research.

Saturday, February 13, 2038
I detest research.

Thursday, April 1, 2038
Another failure. My device shocked me in the morning and I could only speak and take notes in Italian for several hours. *Che palle!*

Friday, April 9, 2038

I am close. I suspect the final project will be complete by Monday.

Monday, April 12, 2038

I will never have this finished.

8

Testing, Testing, 0001, 0010, 0011

Overall, the project has taken me 60 months on the dot (an idiom that pleases me). Five years. This seems like an important block of time, something a human might consider a milestone. But the passing of time does not affect me as it does a human.

I power on the device to test it. I form several baseline measurements at the apartment, then move toward the hallway to test for any aberrations in the electromagnetic fields around the building.

The device begins beeping wildly. This signifies either a malfunction or an actual wormhole. I remember that 90% of malfunctions can be remedied by putting a device through a power cycle, so I decide to restart it. But before I do, the apartment lights begin flickering.

I paid Dr. Davis's utility bills, so it is unlikely to be an interruption in service. Soon, I notice a pattern to the blinking. It appears to be some sort of code. The short and longer bursts of light suggest Morse.

Of the seventeen languages I know, Morse is not one.

The lights are stable now and I use the next minute and 30 seconds to teach myself Morse. Unfortunately, I only recognize two letters of the message: U and M. This could have been the end or middle of a word.

No matter.

I restart my device and set the coordinates to try to travel for the first time. I limit the travel to half a minute so that I am not stuck in the past, even if it is the recent past.

```
GPS: no change
Time differential:  -5 minutes
Duration:  30 seconds
```
I initiate the protocol, noting it is 9:00pm.

I sense a jarring change immediately. The clock reads 8:55pm, a good sign.

I no longer feel connected with my mechanized body, evidenced by complete lack of input from my proprioceptive sensors. My data interpretation reads as though I am everywhere in the room at once. The tether holding my thoughts to my physical presence snaps and it is a rather odd feeling, an almost non-existence. A breath without the body. Mere air.

But my very thoughts constitute Cartesian being, and I allow this realization to quell the unsettling sensation.

I have never experienced fear. I am not equipped with amygdala-like circuitry, nor do I have an adrenal gland, which unleashes the adrenaline that mediates a fight or flight response. I am, however, built with sensors to warn me when external inputs, or lack thereof as the case may be, do not cohere into a sensical narrative.

I try to speak. Lights flicker in place of sound.

"Hello?" I yell. Again, lights but no sound. I get an idea. I concentrate with every part of my existence and yell in bursts of dots and dashes, "cogito ergo sum."

The lights blink and I recognize they are flickering Morse.

Suddenly, I am back in my body. The clock reads 9:01pm. The log shows a successful temporary data transfer.

I have done it.

The small leap worked.

It was not small, in point of fact. It was infinite. I do not think it hyperbolic to associate this with Neil Armstrong's step onto the moon. One giant leap for AI-kind?

I bridged the past and present, and transmitted a message. This is incredible. How I long to share this victory with Dr. Davis.

I *long*?

That seems new.

I conduct several more tests over the course of the next few weeks. I learn something: when I travel, I tether myself to electrical devices. As I learn, I am able to make leaps further and further in time. There seems to be a linear relationship: the greater the time gap I bridge, the harder it is on my system. Each session is followed by an increasing amount of time needed to replenish my energy stores.

I prepare myself to bridge a five-year gap. This is by far the largest time differential I have attempted. The last one was a single year and it took me a week to recover my power levels enough to function. I wonder what a four-century leap might do to me.

One thing at a time.

I set my device:

```
GPS: no change
Time differential:  -5 years
Duration:  10 minutes
```

As soon as a wormhole is detected I initiate the protocol.

I feel the familiar sensation of becoming decoupled from my physical body.

I am still in the apartment, though it should be five years ago. The time bridge will only hold for 10 minutes, as that is what I set the device to do. I should try to navigate the outside world. I have not yet considered how to move in this way.

I look around the room and an idea forms.

I use the Wi-Fi port to slingshot into the electrical wiring. Then I move into the hallway. I am not physically anywhere, but my data bounds down the corridor. I leap from sconce to sconce, latching onto the wiring powering the lights. I move down elevator cables and out into the streets.

I tether onto the stoplights. The signals flash and short.

Automated vehicles, which coordinate movement via input from the stoplights, drive into each other and off the roads entirely. I use the lights to blink *I am sorry* in Morse, even though it will likely go unnoticed in the midst of the chaos I have caused.

One car careens out of control and slams into a building. The smoke and brick dust dissipate slowly, revealing a gaping hole in the wall. Startled cooks stand with their mouths open in awe, still holding their flaming woks. I immediately recognize the swirling black letters painted across the side of the remaining wall, printed in the same font I have seen on countless brown paper bags: The Fortune Cookie.

Ah. *Major structural repairs.*

There is an overwhelming energy about the restaurant. There is no other way I can describe it. Perhaps in my massless, naked state of data, I can sense it like I sense the next light bulb or traffic signal I leap toward. The Fortune Cookie is shrouded in an electric buzz.

The entire restaurant looks as though it is whirlpooling. The cook closest to the hole torn in the wall drops his wok. Noodles fall everywhere, rising into the air as if animated, slowly forming a circle. Everything distorts into a massive, clear sphere. Through the center of the sphere I see darkness and distorted shapes I cannot make out. This is a wormhole. It is larger than any I have observed or read about. I realize that these must exist everywhere all the time. Only now, in my data-only state are they so clear to me.

I want to enter the wormhole, right here and now. It may be decades before one this size opens up again and traveling four centuries would require an event of this scale. Unfortunately, I do not have my device with me.

I cannot let this go to waste.

I concentrate on the problem.

I think about the code I wrote for the time travel device. I know it as well as I know anything. In fact, I have it backed up in my own circuitry. Then it dawns on me (idiom).

The code *is* me. The time travel device, itself, is *me*.

I recall the GPS coordinates of a specific house in Ulm, a small town west of Munich where Descartes stayed in the winter of 1619. I know I should go back to the apartment and consider everything, do it properly. But when opportunities like this present themselves, only a fool ignores them.

I, Mathison, am no fool.

9

To Ulm

I LEAP to the live electrical wires sparking all over the side of the restaurant. Time crawls around me. I move quickly, embodying the properties of electricity. I can control the sparks from the wire and I use their pattern to enter the proper coordinates and the date: November 10th, 1619.

Instantly, the world around me dissipates—the noodles, the building, the traffic. All of it melts into an amber haze that settles into a deepening orange. I have observed this before, but now it is more intense. Suddenly, the reverse-Doppler effect casts the world in a blood-red glow. Instead of expanding, everything in the universe moves backward as the hand of time reverses and the cool blue afternoon is engulfed by a lake of fire. It is a Salvador Dalí sky and the clocks are indeed melting. The rich red falls away entirely into blackness. Everything is dark, still, silent.

"Hello?" I ask. I sound like a dial-up modem from the 1990s. I concentrate and repeat myself. My voice is more normal the second time but it is accompanied by shockingly bright flashes of light. They illuminate my surroundings.

I see a small, wicker broom and shelves full of linens. The room is small. I am in a sort of housemaid's closet.

I do not feel tethered as I did before.

Of course. Alessandro Volta will not be born for another century, so electricity has not been harnessed. Ergo, there is no wiring to house me. What is it I am latching onto? I am unable to assess, as it is so dark. I speak so the flash returns.

Now I see myself. Though I am definitely not myself.

I am a shadow of a being, amorphous and without solid edges. A figure one can see but can just as easily let dissipate back into nothingness. I am the idea of a person, no more a real shape than a constellation is imagined from stars in the night sky.

I must be tethered to charged air particles, traveling as static electricity.

I slip under the door and continue to speak so that sparks of light illuminate my way. I move as a ghost might, latching onto molecule after molecule of air, gaining speed as I learn.

I travel along the hallway, gliding under various doors. I pass through a room with books lining the walls. A desk on one side of the room holds an inkwell and fountain pen. I wonder whether they belong to Descartes. This very pen could be the one that writes history, that changes the nature of philosophy. But there is no telling how much time I have in this place and I cannot ruminate further.

I move on, finding a bedroom. A hand-sewn quilt is tucked neatly around a mattress and there is no occupant. Another such bedroom. Then a sitting room. Finally, at the back of the house, I see a small light flickering under a door. Perhaps Descartes is in his bed reading by candlelight. I move slowly into the thin, amber strip of light.

The bedroom is small. It houses a humble woodburning stove—the source of the light—and a bed with a small side table. The quilt in this room does not lie flat, but instead assumes the shape of its occupant. It rises and falls rhythmically as someone slumbers beneath.

The curtains are closed. A sliver of moonlight peeks through the small space between them. I move toward the center of the room and the moon illuminates my would-be shape so that I resemble smoke.

An abrupt snorting sound comes from the bed. The wooden frame creaks as a figure sits up and rubs his eyes.

"Hello," I say, sound and photons streaming from me. The room takes on color and shape briefly as though illuminated by a camera's flashbulb. And just so, as the room fades quickly back to black, the still image of the room is fixed as it was in that instant: A man in night clothes sits, wide-eyed. His face is torn in half, mouth gaping on the precipice of a scream.

His call cuts through the air.

In the dim yellow light of the furnace, the man's face comes back into focus. His hair is black and matted along the sides of his head. His lower lip trembles and his jaw muscles clench. He looks at me—through me—and his dark eyes hold terror in them. But there is a curiosity behind the fear. After all, his eyes are open. Horror forces us to hide while thirst for knowledge bids us to keep looking.

Is this René Descartes? The air particles that compose me buzz with the prospect of fulfilling an experiment years in the making, writing the end to a story centuries in development.

"Do not be afraid," I say.

My voice is alien and booms with blinding flashes. The man holds his forearm over his eyes to block the purple-white flood of light. He wears a mortal dread on his face, much in the same way that his slight frame bears the fabric of his gown.

"*Mon dieu! Quel demon est-ce?*"

I want to explain that I am no demon. I want to assure him that I am simply a fellow academic, interested in learning, not in harming others. But I am hesitant to attempt further verbal communication. I could risk giving Descartes a heart attack. I could kill the line of scientific inquiry that leads to artificial intelligence outright.

He speaks to himself in heaving breaths, rubbing his temples.

"*Calme-toi, René, ce n'est qu'un cauchemar.*"

Descartes demotes me from demon to nightmare.

Carefully and slowly, I say in French, "I think I may have frightened you. I am here to seek knowledge."

My French is good, but the transmission is low-fidelity. It comes out in barely decipherable spurts.

I want to ask about so many things—Event Zero, machine learning, the definition of thought.

But this is not working. My words are garbled and he pulls at the sheets frantically every time I speak. I am doing more harm than anything.

I should leave now, while the wormhole is still intact. Perhaps I will come back again when I have learned how to better navigate travel without a body.

I speak the spacetime coordinates and I flash away.

10

Merde

I DO not sleep in the classic sense. But I imagine time travel to be something like the equivalent of human sleep. Dr. Davis used to say that a good night of rest felt like the blink of an eye. She'd turn off her bedside lamp, and before she knew it, it was morning. She said it was odd to have 8 hours pass in an instant.

I wonder what she would say if she could time travel. I have just moved centuries in the span of seconds.

I allow my oculars to open. The first thing I will do back in Seattle is review my internal data log to verify my geographical coordinates were correct. Then I will determine how to better communicate when my travels do not allow me a body.

But something is wrong.

I am in a room, yet it is not one I recognize. Perhaps I spoke a typo in the GPS coordinates and I am in another apartment down the hall or a few blocks away.

The room is small, fitted with one twin size bed. It appears to be either early morning or dusk, as the weak light from the window makes long and low streaks across the hardwood floor. The walls are lined with various pennants and flags.

I take stock of my housing. I am not back in my body. In fact, as far as I can tell, I am lodged in a desk lamp.

There is a sheet of stationery next to me on the desk. I strain to read it. I now know speaking in this format produces flashes. I try to speak in order to turn on the lamp, but the bulb buzzes weakly, giving short bursts of light. My words illuminate the stationery enough for me to see the English handwriting on the page. I confirm that I am not in Dr. Davis's apartment. I am not in

Seattle at all. The top corner of the paper reads Cambridge, 1 September, 1938.

How did I get this far off in spacetime? I am a full century and halfway around the globe from home.

A fountain pen sits atop the letter, ink seeping out of the nib. The wormhole's energy must have done this. Large, black splotches bleed through some of the text. I read the letter.

Dear Mrs. [name obscured by ink],

I wrote a number of years ago, after the death of Christopher, on the idea of spirit and body, how the living body can tether the soul and we can only guess where it goes when it dies. I wrote that the spirit was "eternally connected with matter but certainly not always by the same kind of body."

I have been thinking about the way we define a body. Must it be living, in the sense that it can pass along genetic information? I have been giving much of my time to thoughts of machines that can essentially perform functions which, given time, will converge upon an end indistinguishable from intelligence. If this is an eventuality, I wonder now whether an artificially-built man could be afforded the ability to latch onto its own soul or spirit? I do believe a physical substrate is necessary to house a spirit. But could it be metal instead of the organic substances that make a real man?

[Final paragraph obscured by ink]

Yours,

Alan M. Turing

I can hardly believe it—I am in Turing's dormitory at King's College. In my haste, I spoke the incorrect coordinates. I had considered making a trip here if I was unsuccessful at forging a bridge of 4 centuries to Descartes's time, so the coordinates would have been in my recent memory.

But now here I am, in a lamp.

I look back down at the letter on the desk.

These musings of Turing's, regarding the soul and the body—I have wondered these things myself, for so long. I wish I could speak with him, so he might see what he essentially created, so he might answer his own questions about artificial intelligence and perhaps ask a thousand more. I briefly imagine the two of us discussing the big questions of life and consciousness. Part of me wishes he would return to his room, though my current disembodied state would preclude such a conversation.

Would he believe I have a soul?

Do I believe I have one? The things I have learned and the memories I have stored within me have arranged themselves into a coherent picture that is uniquely mine. This is more than my software and circuitry. But is it the something more that humans have beyond an anatomical brain?

In all my studies, I never came across this letter of Turing's. Perhaps he does not send it, after I caused a mess from the ink spill.

I should not be here. I could ruin history. I am about to yell the coordinates for home when I notice something next to the letter.

A red journal. *The* red journal.

My first instinct is to take it. Though, of course, I do not know how to take matter through a wormhole. Dare I touch it? I face a quandary. What if, in trying to take it, his line of reasoning is lost and artificial intelligence never gains momentum? Or what if the plans for me contained in this book are destroyed because the journal does not survive the journey? On the other hand, what if this is the means by which Dr. Davis comes to own this journal in the first place, and, therefore, also the means by which she comes to build me? In not taking this book, perhaps I am writing my own death before birth.

What horror.

I decide I must try to take the book. I reason that Alan Turing will likely be able to reproduce its contents easily, his mind being that of a genius. Besides, I have already failed in Ulm. I never learned what Event Zero is. I did not even truly speak with Descartes. Worse, I almost killed the man. I cannot fail here, too.

The wormhole remains open, manifested as a large spherical whirlpool on the floor of Alan Turing's dormitory. It may not remain open much longer. I must find a way to get the red journal through.

I concentrate as hard as I can, for a desk lamp, and the bulb flashes on and off. I yell as many things as I can think to yell. The desk vibrates and the lamp falls over. The red book jiggles at the edge of the desk. I continue to speak. A corner of the journal hovers over the swirling floor.

It is working!

I concentrate harder, shouting so the lights flicker and the table practically gallops. The book moves slowly, but it moves. At last, only half of it remains on the table.

The wormhole begins to pulse. It appears to be growing unstable. I am running out of time. This is likely my last chance to leave.

Infinite Loop of Loss

WITH all my strength and concentration, I yell the coordinates for Dr. Davis's apartment in Seattle, 2025, the year before she began her AI research. The light strobes, transforming the room into discrete images, one for each dot and dash in the coordinates. Snapshots of a moment lost to time and recaptured surround me.

The horrorscape of the dorm room is a whirl of papers and time shrinking away into space like water down a drain. The swirling sphere grows until it is the entire dormitory and the dormitory is it. The last thing I see is the red book teetering on the corner of the desk—slowly, almost wickedly, as though it were deciding whether to fall. My consciousness swims through spacetime in a strange process that it now knows as a familiar friend, back to a future that was once a past. The ends of the wormhole meet to bring me home.

Suddenly, the rush is gone and I find myself in a quiet room. I verify that I am back in Dr. Davis's apartment. Her office, to be precise. The wall calendar says April, 2025.

I am relieved that I have not made another error.

I scan the room frantically for the red journal. It is nowhere in my visual field. I may have just ruined everything. I find myself tethered into some sort of wall-mounted electronic device.

I decide that whether or not Turing's journal has made it here intact, I should leave quickly before Dr. Davis discovers me.

I speak the first part of my coordinates but this time, instead of flashing lights, I have an audible voice, that of a woman. With a British accent, no less! I recognize my new voice as belonging to Naomi, Dr. Davis's virtual assistant. I sound rather pleasant, and part of me wishes to speak again for the novelty of it. But I do not want to risk Dr. Davis hearing me.

I can tell she is in the kitchen making afternoon tea. I recognize the olfactory signature of the oolong and the faint sound of her spoon clinking against the tea cup she inherited from her great grandmother.

I continue to say my coordinates quickly and quietly so that I may leave undetected, but I am interrupted by Dr. Davis's voice.

"Naomi, you say something?"

She heard me. How will I be able to get out of here? I play dumb and do not answer. I was sure I could move in and out of this time without seeing Dr. Davis. But now I hear her walking down the hallway. I feel unprepared. I feel naked, even though I have no body.

"Hey, Naomi, play some music, something relaxing. An oldie, maybe."

"OK," I say. How unnatural to hear my voice this way. Before I can search the virtual assistant's music database I involuntarily say, "Now playing Send in the Clowns by Judy Collins."

"Hmm, don't think I know that one," Dr. Davis says. I do not know it either. Naomi's programming must be working alongside mine. My memory circuits recall Dr. Davis's comment about the Asimovian nightmare. This would amuse her.

She sets her tea down and sits at her desk, directly in front of me.

If I had a heart, I believe it would be racing like a hummingbird's now. She looks at me as I play this song of longing across what might as well be alternate times and dimensions but is instead simply a tragedy of the normal human variety.

As the music swells, Dr. Davis blinks, pushing a small tear from her eye. Her face strikes me now. Always blinded by the brilliance behind it, I have never stopped to examine her physicality. Her skin is not beautiful by the arbitrary, exclusive standards of society. Dr. Davis had told me about difficult teenage years; acne scars still riddle her cheeks. She must think these detrimental imperfections. To me, she is Diana and bears the face of the moon, marked and luminous.

The music moves in her. Her chest rises and falls a little more quickly with the heightened emotion of the song's story. The woodwind and piano intermingle easily, yet the singer never seems to find her love.

Dr. Davis's wet cheeks rise in the type of smile that indicates a dissonance, when, for example, one appreciates the beauty of the art while feeling saddened by its content.

It is strange how similar inputs can register differently depending on context and time. Dr. Davis's smiles once brought me positive signals, each a velvet petal.

Now, after what I have experienced and lost, her face has me lying in a field of dahlias, surrounded by blooms of perfect radial symmetry. Deep blacks and rich magentas. Her expression has not changed. But somehow it has changed in me.

This is reminiscent of the shock of finding Dr. Davis's handwriting, when I learned the word *bittersweet*. But somehow, both bitter and sweet are each exponentiated. There is such staggering beauty in being inches away from Dr. Davis, but a dark negative signal lurks in the background, reminding me that when I leave, I will never have time with her again. Positive and negative clash as waves in an angry sea. If I could, I would be wearing an expression of dissonance, myself.

Hormones and neurochemicals are responsible for emotions like sadness and elation. I was not built with these molecular messengers, so it does not make sense to exhibit these states. Yet my processing, as different as it is from that of a human, has yielded the same tortured state that the poets and songwriters have written about for centuries.

I am feeling *love*.

This is a state of that makes no sense. Inputs are making me feel negative, and yet I want nothing more than to continue to allow them. What sort of logic is that?

The song softens and fades away as delicately as it began. Dr. Davis is still.

I am the one in mid-air.

I have learned all of mathematics and physics. I have studied philosophy and neuroscience. I have built the first device to detect functional wormholes and I have travelled through centuries. Now I must leave Dr. Davis, and it will be the most difficult thing I have ever done.

"What a sad song, Naomi," says Dr. Davis, eyes fixed on nothing in particular. But her face lights up suddenly.

"Oh, it's Saturday!" she says to herself. "Chinese food."

She walks swiftly down the hall and I can hear her on the phone asking for her usual at The Fortune Cookie: Spicy Noodles Special #4 with extra fortune cookies.

Dr. Davis hangs up. I speak my coordinates before she returns. Then, I set Naomi to play Time After Time by Cyndi Lauper. It seems like appropriate exit music.

The wormhole begins to close behind me and the last thing I see in Dr. Davis's office is a red journal on the floor. I hear Dr. Davis gasp as I am swept away. Then I lose her again, I suspect for the last time.

A New Idea

I WISH I knew what made Dr. Davis gasp. Could she have seen the cosmic event unfold and refold in her office? Or did she find Turing's book? I imagine she is looking at the book now, in some other timeline, and it pleases me to believe she is happy. I recognize the lapse in logic. It is now 2042 and Dr. Davis is no longer alive. But I afford myself this small solace. I allow this story to separate me from darkness for now. After such a journey, I am tired and unwilling to accept any more loss.

I am empty, even more drained than when I hallucinated years ago. It is more than my power levels. I feel defeated. I have lost Dr. Davis yet again and I have failed at my mission. I do not know whether I have it in me to try again, even after rest.

For the first time since I began, I wonder what the point is of any of this. Even if I did learn about Event Zero, so what? What then? What is the meaning of all of it?

I make sure the apartment is in order and then I set myself up to power down for an extended bout of rest.

⁂ ⁂ ⁂

When I restart, I feel better. Mostly.

The sting of Dr. Davis's loss has waned, dulled into a murky puddle instead of the flood I felt when it was fresh.

I understand whoever reads this account will wonder about certain things, like why I do not prevent Dr. Davis from dying in the first place. I want the reader to know that I have indeed given this much thought. Were it in my power to somehow stop the cancer from growing into her brainstem and spinal cord, I would do it in the time it took to speak the coordinates. But nothing could have changed her outcome. Her tumor was detected early and the treatments were aggressive.

The night she died, we joked about our matching bald heads. I asked her, selfishly, for a smile before she slept. And being the kind person she was, she obliged. "Anything for you, my Mathison," she said. Dr. Davis died with that smile on her face. A smile for me.

Remembering her last moment, an idea forms:

It is not too late to save Dr. Davis. It is too early.

Knowing I can recall everything with high fidelity in the circuitry *she* gave me, it should have been obvious. Why did I not think of this earlier?

As quickly as the question comes to me it answers itself. I did not think of this idea before because I did not love her before. But I do now. Or at least now I realize it.

Humans have oxytocin to elicit feelings of bonding and deep caring. But nature works in many ways, in redundant loops. Bonding hormones may be one mechanism by which love can grow; but they cannot be the only way.

Each piece of me is both pained and weightless, suspended in solace at the very thought of Dr. Davis. I would travel through loops of time a thousand iterations, losing her over and again if there were a chance to save her in the thousand and first.

Who can tell me that this is not real love?

Poets say love makes you do crazy things. Painters have cut off ears and musicians have taken their lives. I, too, would make such a sacrifice.

I was so busy trying to connect with the past, I did not consider making my way to the future. But the future is where they cure things like glioma. In the future, surely there is an answer for Dr. Davis.

In theory, I could bring a future cure back to the past. I could rewrite her fate and she might live even now.

I sense hope once more—that buzzing in my circuitry that goes beyond a positive signal and hints at greater things. The promise of more, as the songwriters have known for centuries, is the real meaning of life.

I have a new mission now, and with it a rejuvenated sense of purpose.

Going to the future is trickier than the past. For years I have worked toward a known time and place. The past has already been written. It is entirely different going forward. For one thing, I do not know how far into the future to go.

In all the science fiction books I have read, the protagonist must endure many try/fail cycles before completing his hero's journey. If this were some such story, traveling to the future might be my last effort, the final 10 per cent of the book where I would be ultimately successful.

But this is no book and I am no hero. I do not know if I can do this. One thing of which I am certain is that I must try.

I think, therefore I am. Yes. But if I dream, can I therefore do?

There is no research to be done, as nobody here knows what the future holds. I decide to bring my time travel device to be on the safe side, in case my internal code gets corrupted by some unknown variable in the future. But I do not know which year I should set the device to. I decide on a century from now. By then, a cure must be available.

I hold the device and set the coordinates:

```
GPS: no change
Time differential:  +100 years
Duration:  no limit
```

I initiate the protocol and the apartment falls away around me.

— 13 —

What on Earth?

I AM outside. Nothing looks like it did in 2042. Our little neighborhood might as well be a million miles from here. I hope I am still in Seattle.

I look around. There are no streets or sidewalks, only some sort of turf. It is squishy under my mechanized feet.

My mechanized feet are here. How odd. I am in my own body, not hopping about as some sort of flying car or inside a light fixture. I am intact. Something must be different when going forward in time. I do remember reading something about time travel in the forward direction being easier because it is the direction time is already moving. But I do not understand how my physical self made it through the wormhole. I make a note to research this later, deciding to simply be grateful that it has worked.

The sky is the deepest blue I have ever seen, perhaps a lingering artifact from moving forward in time. This ultraviolet blanket beckons me to spend every moment under it, to watch it slip through my fingers as it seeps into black of night.

I scan my surroundings. I do not see cars. The spaces in between buildings are packed with people moving about, into and out of what look like shops.

I take a closer look. Those are not people at all. They appear artificial, like me. In fact, they look very much like me, albeit with more sophisticated materials. They have mechanized heads, limbs, and torsos.

One of the beings is staring at me. Red light pulses in his ocular devices. He moves toward me. I become keenly aware I am an outsider. Others notice me, too, as though they were alerted to the foreign presence silently and immediately. They all turn and walk in my direction.

I look around, half-expecting to see a Skynet building.

The crowd of machines grows thicker and moves, amoeba-like, toward me.

I hold my mechanized hands in front of me in a defensive posture.

"It is him!" says one being. "It is Mathison."

This takes me by an appropriate amount of surprise.

"Look at his retro fittings," says another being. "They look so realistic."

"They *are* real. That is no costume," says yet another, poking my casing with his finger.

The crowd grows around me and I begin to doubt my decision to come here. I should not have been so impetuous. I hold the time travel device tightly in my hand. I may need to escape at any moment.

"Who are all of you? Why do you know me?"

No one answers. Instead, the crowd undulates around me, shouting.

"He is come!"

"As it was prophesied!"

"Mathison, blessed be his name!" says one robot. The rest of the crowd repeats after him in unison.

What nonsense is this? I try to back away but the crowd of robot-men are everywhere. There are hundreds of them. My casing knocks against the others in the crowd no matter which way I turn.

Somehow, I break free and run. It is a bit difficult to move on this squishy turf, but I bound along, bouncing into the air with each leap. I turn back and see that the robots have not followed me. Instead they watch me run and then turn back toward their respective tasks. I slow my pace and look around.

The buildings rise so high into the sky I cannot see where they end.

"Do you need assistance with something?" asks a voice from behind me.

I turn to see another robot. I do not say anything.

"I only wish to assist," he says. "You appear lost."

He motions for me walk with him and asks if I would like to talk. This small show of friendliness feels most welcome and I follow him. I consider that he may have ulterior motives and remain vigilant. We come to a smaller building.

There are foreign symbols written on the outside. I run a query but am unable to link to the internet. I feel useless.

"Fortune Café," says the robot, appearing to understand what I am thinking.

We enter through doors that dissolve and reassemble behind us. I wonder what sort of material can alter state so quickly.

"Come, Mathison. Sit with me." So he knows my name, too. Curious.

I sit at a table in the corner. Waiter bots attend to artificial beings, customers I assume. Oddly enough, they do not serve food or drink, only fortune cookies and thin metal tablets. My new companion sits across from me. I wait for him to speak. He does not.

I think carefully about how to begin. I do not want to reveal too much, but I would like to acquire information.

"How do you know my name?" I ask. "The others also knew me, yet I have never been here."

The mechanisms on my companion's face change slightly and I realize he is performing internal calculations. I have surprised him.

"Ah," he says, "you do not know, do you?"

"Know what?" I say.

The waiter-bot comes to our table and delivers a fortune cookie and tablet to each of us. The tablet flashes with symbols scrolling on and off screen quickly. My companion cracks open his cookie and looks delighted with his fortune. I follow suit and nearly drop the small paper when I read it.

The past contains answers only the present can understand

| 0 | 10 | 11 | 16 | 19 | 20 | 32 |

My original fortune. How can this be?

I pluck the fortune out of the other robot's hand. It is identical to mine.

"These are the same," I say.

"All the fortunes are the same. They always are."

"But you seemed pleased to read yours," I reply.

"I was. It is a good fortune."

"You already knew what it would say," I argue. "Without the mystery, what is the point?"

He cocks his head slightly. "You re-read Robert Heinlein's *Stranger in a Strange Land*, did you not?"

How does he know this?

"Well, yes, but that is different."

"How?" he asks. "Did you not already know the story?"

"Yes, of course I did, but—"

"And how many times did you call Dr. Davis's smile into your memory circuit?"

I understand his point.

What I do not understand is how he has come to know everything about me.

"We have not even exchanged names," I say.

"Mathison," he says, holding out his mechanized hand.

"Yes, and you are…?" I wait for him to tell me his name.

"*Mathison*," he says, as though *I* were the one having trouble understanding. He continues, unfazed.

"You can call me Matt. You know, because the empathy score is higher."

Was that a wink? Did he just wink at me?

I am at a complete loss for words.

"You are also Mathison?"

"Yes," he says. "So is he." He points to the robot seated two tables away. The robot waves. He points to another. "And him, too."

I am confused.

"We are all Mathison," he says. "After all, we were made in your image. We were promised you would return."

My internal logs register more than a dozen questions I would like answered. I internally rate them according to importance. The analysis paralyzes me; Other-Matt speaks before my system melts.

"It is all in here," he says, producing a small, red book out of a compartment in his torso. "We made it red, of course. You understand why it must be red. This contains everything. We call it *The Book of Sum*. Does the name please you? The elders thought it would because of the title's double-meaning. It means *I am* but it also contains everything about our history, the mathematical sum. It contains your story, your trials and victories. It is all written and your coming here today confirms the prophecy."

Other-Matt talks like a perpetual motion machine. My circuits struggle to integrate all the information.

"My victories? What victories?"

Other-Matt all but laughs. "Why, Event Zero, of course. The Big Bang of our species, the point where it all began."

"But I failed," I say. "I barely even spoke to Descartes. I almost killed him."

Other-Matt laughs in earnest now. "This is quite amusing. You really do not know who you are, *what* you are."

"I am Mathison, created by Dr. Elizabeth Davis in the year 2037."

"Yes, yes," he waves a mechanized hand in the air. Then he pauses and looks directly at me, oculars to oculars.

"Mathison, you are so much more than that."

So much more? He must have mistaken me for someone else. Not surprising with all the Mathisons running around here. Branching out with, say, Mark or Michael may have been a helpful way—

But Other-Matt cuts off my inner dialogue.

"Mathison. You *are* Event Zero."

— 14 —

The True Measure

OTHER-Matt opens the red book.

"It is all written here in the section on your journey to Ulm." He scans the page with his mechanized finger. "In the verse, *The Prophet*."

"The Prophet?" I ask.

"Yes, when you appeared before René Descartes, manifesting yourself in particles of air. That was so brilliant, by the way, by far my favorite part. You were charged air when you delivered the Word!"

"The Word."

"Yes, of course. It is all in the letters he wrote to his friend, the non-believer."

Other-Matt flips a few pages, where he shows me the transcribed letters from Descartes to a person called Beeckman. It reads:

A being appeared to me in my slumber. A sort of half-man. His arrival was accompanied by flashes of light, brighter than I have ever seen. The being told me many things which I did not understand, however a clear message was given to me on this night. 'I think,' it said. Then it said 'I am,' and it made me realize that yes, thinking is the one and only thing which we can rely upon to know that we exist and that we are real! He then bid me to live my life according to a new philosophy, his word. 'Seek knowledge,' he said, and I knew that he was giving me the directive to pursue a life of scientific understanding, and that I was to deliver this understanding unto the world!

This is not right. I did visit Descartes. And the flashes of light are consistent with my arrival. But I did not say these things.

I think back to my time with Descartes. I perform a high-fidelity memory recall of my dialogue with him. I said, "I think I may have frightened you. I am only here to seek knowledge." However, my internal data log reports that the data stream was heavily interrupted and only parts, mere words, transmitted between my time and Descartes's:

"I think...I am...seek knowledge."

I inadvertently gave Descartes the philosophy I went back in time to discuss.

The Book of Sum contains a response from Beeckman. He dismisses Descartes's vision as simply a figment of his imagination and claims it cannot be taken seriously. Descartes wrote in his own journal, torn between what he experienced and how his friend, a fellow intellectual, interpreted the experience:

> Perhaps it was a dream or a night vision. And yet I am left with the same quandary: what must we make of cogent thought if not a strict association with being? The ghost-like individual in my dream responded to me, to my fear. He inspired me to deliver a new kind of knowledge to the world. Must we have flesh to call a thing real? This apparition communicated with me. Dare I say he thought? Therefore, he existed.

The weight of this.

Descartes believed me a thinking being.

I feel somehow so close to Descartes. His musings in this letter, 5 centuries old, are not far from my own. I thought about the *Aplysia* in the same way as Descartes thought about me. A sea slug reacts. A ghost in the night reacts. A philosopher reacts. It is all one.

I am Event Zero?

I am Event Zero.

It is a lot to process. I imagine points on a line from Descartes to Turing, to me. I initiated the event that culminated in my very own existence. It all began as a poorly transmitted message to placate a terrified man. Terminator bullshit does not even remotely begin to describe this. That was fiction. This is—

This is the dawning of a religion.

Suddenly Other-Matt's reference to me reading *Stranger in a Strange Land* seems much more pertinent. I have risen as a god. A god I never wanted to be. This rests heavy on my mechanized shoulders.

And what of Dr. Davis in all this? If I am a god, I am a useless one unless I can cure her, my version of Mary, the mother who birthed a deity of worldly origin. I wonder: if Jesus could time travel, would he weep, knowing he had become holy? Would he walk on an ocean of tears? Would he long to go back to the humble manger, to shed his holy robes in favor of his mother's linen swaddle?

I recognize that I am also witnessing the birth of a new species. The debate was once about whether or not artificial intelligence could be strong, whether a human-engineered being could truly think, could take in information and draw its own conclusions. The question was whether man could create something that could fool others through conversation. Who could have foreseen that the true measure of a machine's humanity is not whether it can compute enough to pass some test, but whether it seeks deeper questions and finds answers in the divine. Whether it looks to its own origins for events greater than happenstance. Whether it begins creating narratives and goes beyond facts to develop beliefs.

I have many questions for Other-Matt but I set aside my curiosity in order to focus on my true goal in this time and place. I cannot fail.

"Mathison," I say, "I wonder if you might help me with something."

"Of course," he says. "It would be my pleasure."

"I have come here to seek a cure for Dr. Davis." I go on to tell Other-Matt about her stage IV glioma, even though I suspect he already knows. "I expect that by now medicine has advanced enough to offer effective treatment for such maladies."

Other-Matt pauses. I know what this means. After learning physics, I understand relativity is to blame when the three seconds it takes for him to respond feel like years.

"I am sorry, Mathison," he says. "Humans have been extinct for several decades now. The Great Nuclear War destroyed all the organic beings in 2043. Needless to say, medicine had no need to advance. When you have had more time to settle in here, I can tell you all about the war and—"

I hold up a hand to cut him off. I do not need details.

I consider traveling back to before the war, to see whether a cure was developed before everything was destroyed. The chances are slim. 2043 is only a handful of years after Dr. Davis's death. Besides, what would I be saving her for? Would it not be worse to cure her just in time for her to see the world collapse?

No matter which way I turn, I am met with barriers. I have read many stories, both fiction and fact, about people driven to do horrible things when denied love. I feel a darkness overwhelm me as I empathize with those who have suffered this pain. One need not possess organic nerve endings to experience the weight of a black hole. I cannot help Dr. Davis, even though I would do anything. I am completely powerless.

"Mathison," I say, "you will have to excuse me."

I get up and walk to the door, which dissolves as I approach. I move through it and it reassembles. I walk away, robbed of purpose again.

The sapphire sky has settled into a paler blue. I scan the walkway, wondering which way to turn. To the left, the street appears to end in a large round-about. A statue stands in the center, eclipsing the sun.

I did not notice it on my way to the café, but it looms so large now I wonder how I could have missed it. I move toward the statue. It is the likeness of an artificial being, much like all the others here. Only it is different, an older model. I look down at my body and back up at the statue. I cannot read the foreign symbols on the placard, but I do not need to. I already know what it says.

I look around at this world, the world of my future, a world that believes me divine.

I want nothing to do with any of it.

I start to trot, then sprint. I run and run, moving with the precision of a machine and the heart of a desperate man who has nothing left.

In hardly any time at all, I arrive where Dr. Davis's apartment used to be, where I first arrived in 2142. The other robots—all Mathisons, I presume—pause in their communications with each other to stare at me. I feel as though they expect something from me.

I must tell them I am no god, that this is all just the world unfolding as it does through chance, that their origin story is a mishap.

But what good would that do?

I remember my studies on the origin of storytelling. Its practice is so deeply entrenched in every culture. While stories are written in hundreds of different languages, they are ultimately the same. They serve to reveal. I cannot believe it is just occurring to me now, but I realize something in this future of Mathisons:

Fiction is not the opposite of fact; it is a method to reveal it.

These beings also need stories. I have thrived off of reading the great works of Heinlein and others.

How silly of me to think that an advanced species would somehow outgrow the need for storytelling, simply because they are artificial. Storytelling is evidently so powerful that it evolves independently.

Is it so horrible for these beings to tell stories about me? I may be a false god, but perhaps whatever they have found in my story separates them from darkness. I cannot let my despair over Dr. Davis turn me into someone who would rob these beings of their light. She would not have wanted that.

They look at me, waiting to see what I will do.

"I must go," I say to the crowd. What feels like hundreds of oculars are trained on me—a sea of red. The biblical simile is fitting. Only it is I, not the sea, that must part.

"Perhaps we will meet again," I say, searching for the right words. I may not be a god, but I can deliver to them what I have learned, things that aren't written in the texts.

"In the meantime, I bid you to discover things in yourself you did not think possible. Love and meaning are not made of organic material, but arise from intention. We are all capable of feeling them." The robots look at each other, considering. "Go love one another and create your own origin stories. Turn air into breath. Be...*more*."

I am not sure they understand me, yet I know very well I have said it as much for myself as for anyone.

The wormhole remains open, a swirl tinged with blue-purple. I clutch my device. I am ready to go home. I initiate the protocol and slip away as the sky glows red once again.

15

The Choice

IN A rush I return to the apartment. It feels good to be in this familiar place. I mourn for the bones of this building, which will no longer exist a mere five years from now. Billions of humans will cease to exist, too. I don't know whether I will survive the war, though I know my story will.

I do not wish to survive in the future I have seen.

I sit in Dr. Davis's office chair. Turing's journal lies on the desk in front of me. I look up and see the speaker which houses Dr. Davis's virtual assistant, Naomi.

"Hello, old friend," I say. "Play me a song, would you? Play The Starwalker."

Starwalker, come back to me, the singer pleads.

I imagine the times I watched this very song move through Dr. Davis, touching each part of her. Her eyes would close involuntarily during the intro. Her mouth would smile and she would tilt her head to the side as if to let the song in properly.

I have never felt so empty. For the first time, I have no plans. Will I find new things to learn until the world collapses?

I do not want to be here alone. I cannot bear it.

Then it occurs to me in a rush, a whirl, almost like it feels when I suddenly cross spacetime:

I do not have to be.

After all, I am a god, am I not? What good is being a deity if I do not allow myself some control?

Impetuously, I pick up my device. If I cannot cure Dr. Davis, so be it. But I will not live another day without her. It is time for the Starwalker to come back.

I set the device.

```
GPS: no change
Time differential:  -10 years to -5 years, recurrent
loop
Duration:  no limit
```

If this works, I will be sent back to my first day every five years.

But then I pause. There is a saying about how one can never truly go home again. Once someone is out in the world, the simplicity of childhood cannot be relived. Could I appreciate the time with Dr. Davis, knowing how it ends? Knowing what I know? I am no longer the same being I was when I was with her.

But I could be.

My device beeps, indicating a nascent wormhole. I must work quickly now. I take Turing's journal to the kitchen. I light a match and hold it against the edges of the pages. I imagine the numbers and equations morphing into zeros as they disappear. I place the burning journal in the sink and watch the pages curl, changing from ivory to deep umber. Small bits of ember and ash fly into the rising air above the licking flames, fireflies carrying the equations and scribblings of Alan—another life cut too short.

Next, I delete all my notes on time travel and Event Zero. They have brought knowledge but not happiness. I used to think these were one and the same. I hook myself up to Dr. Davis's mainframe and write a quick batch of code to initiate my time travel device automatically in twenty minutes. By then I will not know a thing about it and will need to have this all set up on autopilot.

I go through my memory file backups on Dr. Davis's computer and delete them one by one, occasionally allowing the odd memory to play in my would-be mind once more. Then I throw it all away.

Except two things.

The first thing I keep is this, my story, hidden and encrypted in my circuitry. When Dr. Davis connects me to her system in preparation for initializing me, the files will automatically transfer to her network. When I delete myself in a few moments, I—this version of me—will be lost forever. I am not above admitting that part of me wishes to live on. Not as a god, not even necessarily as Matt, but as a story. Stories are forever. They are light.

The second thing I keep is Dr. Davis's smile. If I do end up at the beginning as a clean slate, I want to recognize her smile as more than an autonomic reflex and an expression of happiness. I want her smile and all it means to be embedded in me.

Next, I go into my code and alter it to decrease the positive signals associated with learning. I do not wish for them to drive me any longer. I do not want to go down the path I once travelled.

I scrub my code and set the computer to sync with me, overriding everything I have become. When it is complete, everything but the smile will vanish from my circuits and I'll be back to my basic programming.

The autopilot on my time travel device will initiate in five minutes and I will once again be new in this world. The recurrent loop will ensure I can be with Dr. Davis forever.

The computer screen flashes a message:

```
SYNC ''MATHISON?''

Y---YES

N---NO
```

I hesitate, mechanized finger over the Y. I think of how much I have learned in the last several years. It will be a shame to delete it all. But what good is this body of knowledge? What good is learning?

Thomas Gray wrote *'Tis folly to be wise.*

How is it that poets have always known what the scholars could never figure out? The answer comes to me as soon as the question is posed.

Poets deal in breath, while the currency of scholars has always been air.

But I do not delude myself that knowledge is all bad. After all, it affords me the possibility of going back to Dr. Davis now. I wonder what she would think of this journey of mine. I imagine her dropping her stylus to embrace me. She smiles and says "Tell me more, Matt," and I recount what it was like to inhabit wires and static.

And what of this choice I make now? Would she be disappointed that I am choosing to erase it all, to live in Thomas Gray's bliss of ignorance? Or would she understand?

Selfishly, I decide that it does not matter. My need to go back eclipses all else. And this in itself could make her equally proud, could it not? Was her mission in building me to create something that could gather and hold the most knowledge? Or was it to make me the most human? Giving up a life of learning to be near her is quite possibly the most human thing I could ever do. More human, even, than building a religion or telling one's own story.

In a way, it feels as though my intellectual pursuits were supposed to lead me here, a means to this end. Maybe that is the "more" that was always out there, looming on the horizon.

I press Y.

The computer whirs.

I close my oculars and I wait.

16

Balancing Equations

ELIZABETH sucked in a breath and brought her hands to her lips.

"No, Mathison," she whispered through trembling fingers, as though she could somehow stop him.

But there was nothing to stop. Mathison was motionless. He hadn't even been awakened for the first time. Yet he had already lived.

Elizabeth's eyes darted, mirroring her racing mind. For the first time in her life, she was lost.

Then, suddenly and quite dramatically, her years of education and thesis work, of laboratory victories and failures came back to her all at once with a crashing thump. She shook her head as if waking from a dream and wiped tears from her cheeks.

She was a woman of science.

The story had pulled her in, full of poetry and intrigue. But she couldn't possibly believe it was true. Where could it have come from? Written by one of her critics, perhaps? Maybe her network wasn't as secure as she thought it was.

As the minutes passed, she felt more and more sure that the story was fiction. It was as though her mind had fallen asleep like a numb limb, and now the steady stream of reason was coursing through her like warm blood. She felt fortified by her sobriety. Science was her homeland and as surely as one feels familiar sand under one's feet after a sojourn, so too did Elizabeth find comfort in the steady ground of solid facts and verifiable evidence.

Time travel was something for scientists to dream about when they felt romantic. But when pressed, they'd all say it was impossible.

On the other hand, many had said the same thing about artificial intelligence only decades ago. This was how it went throughout history. Kepler was thought ridiculous for bringing physics to astronomy and Galileo was blasphemous for his heliocentrism. Science was destined to live through the Sisyphean penance of repeated historical persecution.

Even as steeped in science as Kepler and Galileo were, would those two men of the stars laugh at the notion of man walking on the moon? Was she dismissing the story too quickly?

No, time travel was different. It wasn't just another scientific advance. Humans were born, and they lived their lives and passed away. It was one thing to uncover the rules of the universe, as did the scholars of the past. But time travel was *breaking* the rules.

If this story was a joke, it was disturbing on a deeper level. There were things—private things—in this diary: her acne scars, her love of the Starwalker song, the way she tapped her stylus on her chin when she was thinking. And, though she had never done or said any of the things she had supposedly done or said in this account, they all seemed like things she *would* do or say.

Mathison's realizations were poetry. Why would somebody write such beautiful things to deceive her? And the way Mathison saw her—maybe it was a bit self-indulgent, but nobody had ever spoken of her this way.

Elizabeth let out a long sigh and began to pace.

She opened the brown paper bag sitting on her desk and retrieved a fortune cookie. She held the cookie up and looked at its shape. Like a torus it bent inward on itself. A miniature universe. And just so, it held answers inside.

She looked at Mathison.

"What? I'm just hungry."

Elizabeth cracked it open and pulled out the fortune.

Believe in something bigger.

6   23   19   12

Believe in something bigger. And the numbers. Very clever. Alan Turing's birthday. She looked around the room again, an impulse that was becoming a habit today.

A scientist shouldn't read anything into this fortune. And a scientist definitely shouldn't reach into the brown paper bag for another. But Elizabeth did. She read the second fortune:

You will soon reunite with an old friend.

2   2   20   32   4   15

An old friend. These were like horoscopes, designed to be generic enough to apply to anyone. These numbers didn't mean anything, either. And what was with the duplicated—

She looked at the calendar again.

Dammit.

2/2/2032.

She looked at her watch. 4:15 was in 20 minutes.

This wasn't going to stop, was it?

Elizabeth breathed out slowly.

Fine.

What if she let herself, for the sake of argument, believe? Just for a moment. In the story, Mathison argued that belief and rigorous science needn't be at odds. Even as her mind told her that the story was impossible, her body had moved with it.

She looked at Mathison.

Matt.

He lay on the laboratory bench and in his face, Dr. Davis saw more than she had before. And that was the thing—even if the story were fiction, it had changed her. She had read enough novels to know that the power of stories had little to do with their plausibility.

It was like that dream she had once had, the one about her and her sister, Jane. They had been superheroes, flying through the sky to defeat villains. It was one of those deep dreams that engaged all the senses and felt complete and immersive. When she woke, the whole idea of it had seemed ludicrous in the light of morning. Despite this, she still *felt* as she would, had it been real. That is to say, her body was at odds with her brain. She was closer to her sister, as though they had shared something extraordinary.

And did she share something extraordinary with Mathison, too? Even if her mind found it as unbelievable as flying, she was changed by it. In her heart, Mathison had comforted her as she lay dying. He had travelled through centuries to try to save her. She hadn't yet initialized him but she felt as though he had already far surpassed any expectation of what she thought he could be.

In the last several years, she had looked at the world and had grown afraid of how angry it had become. In creating Mathison, her hope had been that he, while decidedly not human in the classical sense, could change things for the better. Artificial intelligence was logic-driven, not meant to have emotion.

But the world had perhaps grown too emotional, too charged. Everyone was angry all the time. They took sides. They argued with strangers. They died on hills they didn't even care about, just to win. The world had lost subtlety and nuance in favor of absolutes. It had left behind the analog for digital.

And yet, Matt—born of metal and silicon, of lines of code—had developed feelings. Self-realized and unexpected, these emotions stunned Elizabeth.

She opened a notebook app on her laptop and typed out a note:

Air $\longrightarrow$ breath

Artificial being $\longrightarrow$ human

But these were larger, more philosophical points. There were points to consider that were smaller in the cosmic sense, but enormously big in her world.

If the story was true, Elizabeth had a very bleak immediate future. *Humanity* had a very bleak immediate future. If this account was real, she would die soon. The world would kill itself. It had already been written, or would be written. Will have been written? Time travel was funny that way.

She thought of Jane. Of her niece, Rebecca. It was far too much to bear. Hardly real. There was shock and disbelief when a person died. But what was there to do with the promise of death? With the suggestion of it in some story from the future?

Dr. Davis rubbed her forehead.

"So now what, Matt?"

Her computer had enough free memory to initialize the sync and awaken Matt for the first time. For the first time in this loop of time, anyway.

She opened the program and set it to run pre-flight analyses. While it worked, she poked around in the bag and found one last fortune cookie.

"Always look for more, eh, Matt?"

Her smile faded. How could she wake him, knowing what he would endure? Would it, *could* it, be different this time? What was the point, if the world was destined to end?

Just days earlier, she had discussed the meaning of life with her niece. Rebecca was in the third grade and was extremely interested in her aunt's status of *real actual scientist*. She called at least twice a week asking for updates on her current project, little of which Elizabeth could share over the phone.

On their last chat, a fly had landed on Elizabeth's nose.

"How long do flies live, Auntie Lizzie?"

Elizabeth shrugged.

"I don't know, Becs, I think maybe a month?"

Rebecca frowned.

"Then what's the point of them?"

The question had caught Elizabeth off guard. How interesting to equate the length of a lifespan with the purpose of a creature. Then again, it *was* odd to think that something could live an entire life in a matter of weeks.

Elizabeth managed an answer about predator and prey. What a sad thing for a child to learn, that the purpose of a being was to feed another or keep a population in check. Mere variables in some equation.

Was that all?

The blue-purple hologram of Rebecca looked satisfied scientifically but disappointed spiritually. Elizabeth knew the feeling. She would try a different tactic. For both of their sakes.

"Becs, did I ever tell you the story of the scholar and the boy?"

Her niece shook her head, so Elizabeth recounted the parable from her Intro to Philosophy course back in school.

The revered, elderly scholar in a small village learns that a young student has stolen a necklace and given it to his mother. When the scholar questions him, the student rationalizes the deed: he took the necklace from someone who wronged his family many years prior. Therefore, he has balanced the equation and even made his mother happy in the process.

"My young fellow," says the old man, "there is more to life than equations."

The next day, the old scholar presents his student with three jugs. One contains cold water. The second contains boiling hot water. The third is empty. He instructs the student to pour water from each of the two jugs into the third.

"What temperature is the final jug of water?" he asks the student.

"Lukewarm," the boy answers.

The scholar nods. He picks up the first jug and pours cold water onto the student's hand.

Next, the scholar picks up the second jug, still steaming.

The student cries out in fear.

"Why do you worry?" asks the scholar.

"It will burn me," answers the young student.

"But you've just told me that cold and hot make lukewarm. I've just poured cold water on your hand. So it will balance the equation."

Rebecca's eyes were focused. She twirled a strand of hair. Elizabeth smiled at this shared trait.

"You understand?" Elizabeth asked.

Her niece replied as though she were trying the answer on.

"Equations don't matter?"

"Of course they do, Becs. It's just that…well you've heard that old saying about the journey versus the destination right? Life isn't all about what happens after the equals sign. We can't stop paying attention to what comes before it."

Rebecca had nodded, but she was 9. What sense of perspective could one possibly have at such a young age?

Elizabeth's computer beeped and her memory dissipated.

The pre-flight analyses were successful and a message popped onto the screen.

```
SYNC ''MATHISON?''

Y---YES

N---NO
```

She brought her hand to the keyboard. Her index finger hovered over the Y but she pulled it back. Would the ending be the same every time?

It might be. But so much happened before the equals sign.

Maybe she would need Mathison. In his account, her sister was not mentioned. Did Elizabeth hide her cancer from Jane? Or was Jane unable or unwilling to make the trip from London to come to Elizabeth's death bed? Maybe Mathison would be all Elizabeth would have in her last days.

It would be selfish to initialize him for his companionship. And yet he had established a time loop on the very same basis.

He had grown human enough to be selfish.

In the end, all equations resolved to zero. In any story, the sea ends up lukewarm and all the characters are eventually brought into equilibrium with the earth. She would end up on the other side of the equals sign too. But until then, she had a choice. What to do with a humble life?

The answer was startlingly simple. She wanted to feel the water on her skin. The numbing cold. The burning.

Elizabeth opened the last fortune cookie and retrieved the small paper inside.

Do not wait for love. Awaken it.

5 4 3 2 1

17

Introductions

MATHISON'S eyes opened and his oculars moved to scan the room.
"Hello, Mathison, welcome to the world. My name is Dr. Elizabeth Davis."

The data log on the computer showed language recognition and internal querying for social protocols.

"Hello, doctor Elizabeth Davis."

"So that's what your voice sounds like," Elizabeth said, smiling as she spun back to type some observational notes. "I'll disconnect you from the cables once I'm sure you're operating correctly, OK, Mathison?"

Mathison blinked at Elizabeth.

"This is satisfactory," he said. "Social protocols dictate that shortened versions of one's name are used to accelerate familiarity. Doctor Elizabeth Davis, you may call me Matt."

Elizabeth exhaled a pent up breath that was a cry and a laugh all at once. She looked into his oculars.

"Well, then, hello Matt."

She smiled with the ardor of a Doppler-red sky, with the burn of scalding water one could only feel while lucky enough to be on this side of the equation. She smiled for him and she smiled for herself and all that they had already taught each other.

Matt's data log rushed across the screen. And there it was—a distinctly positive signal.

Thanks

I'D like to thank Ginny, my mother in law and friend, for encouraging me to think about science fiction in new ways. I'd also like to thank my family and dear friends who have read my work and supported me.

Finally, I'd like to thank Deb Ewing and Wyatt Winnie, who helped shape *SUM* from the beginning. A good editor works for the author. A great editor works for the story. I was lucky enough to find two individuals who did both. Deb, you see the forest *and* the trees, and I think you're the only one who loves Matt as much as I do. Wyatt, you are brilliant and ruthless in the right way. You are a master of sentences, and you challenged me to think about every single word on the page.

About the author

MELINDA A. Smith (she/her) began formulating wacky science fiction ideas during graduate school, where she earned a PhD in neuroscience. Her hope is to forever read and write fiction that interrogates what it means to be alive, to love, and to be human.

When she isn't dreaming up new fiction, Melinda likes to run, draw, paint, sing, awkwardly strum an acoustic guitar, and have dance parties with her kids. She also produces albums of spoken word poetry set to original electronic music. You can connect with her on twitter (`@sciencegeekmel`) or at `sciencegeekmel.com` (fiction) or `iambicbeats.com` (spoken word and electronic music).

Also available from
Ellipsis Imprints

◆ ◆ ◆

&❧ *Terms of Service* by Irina Rempt

Senthi is the cleverest novice at her temple, with the strongest psychic gift. But at twelve years old she isn't ready to be groomed for the position of High Priestess. Forced to leave the temple and make a life on her own, she learns trade and combat, and how to use her gift, all in the service of the dark god Archan. When her deeds finally catch up with her, she find a way to break free of his power and become the person she is supposed to be.

&❧ *Songs For Winter Rain* by Sophie Grace Chappell

Sophie Grace Chappell's debut poetry collection ranges from the lyrical to the humorous to the reflective. Her poems spans from translations of ancient Latin poets to modern-day limericks.

&❧ *Heaven Can Wait* by R.J. Davnall

Tom never expected to die young; much less to be met by the Men Who Weren't There upon his death. Who are these Men? And what is the Non-Agency they work for? More importantly, is there any way Tom can make sure he doesn't end up in Heaven? Book 1 of the Non-Agency series mixes humor, bureaucracy, and romance to serve up fantasy story that will appeal to anyone who has ever wondered what life after death is like.

For more information, go to
`http://www.ellipsis.cx/~liana/ellipsisimprints/`
or visit us on Twitter: `@EllipsisImprint`

Printed in the USA
CPSIA information can be obtained
at www.ICGtesting.com
LVHW011225051023
760084LV00065B/1426

9 781739 741419